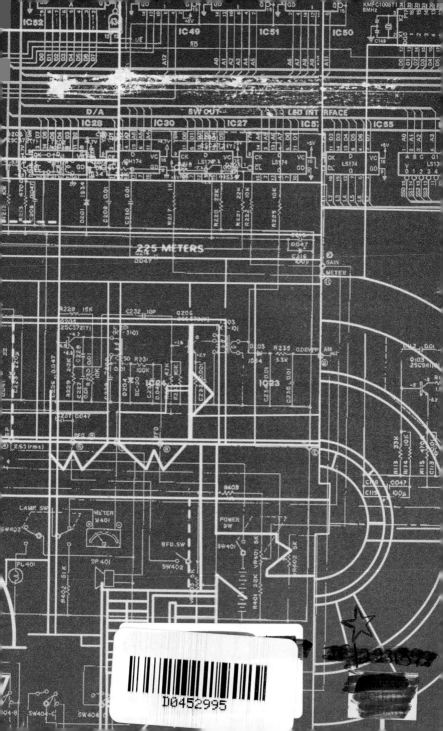

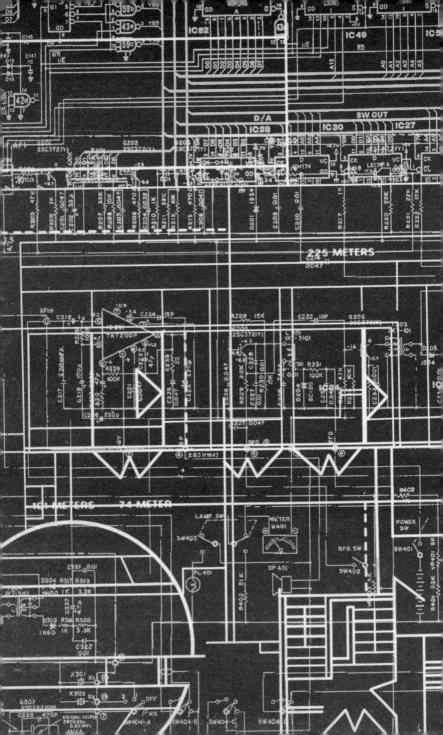

EGMONT

EGMONT

We bring stories to life

First published in Great Britain 2011
by Egmont UK Limited
239 Kensington High Street
London W8 6SA

Written by Barry Hutchison

ISBN 978 1 4052 6101 2

50050/1

Printed and bound in Great Britain

The Forest Stewardship Council (FSC) is an international,
non-governmental organisation dedicated to promoting
responsible management of the world's forests. FSC operates
a system of forest certification and product labelling that
allows consumers to identify wood and wood-based products
from well managed forests.

For more information about Egmont's paper buying policy,
please visit www.egmont.co.uk/ethicalpublishing.
For more information about the FSC,
please visit their website at www.fsc.org

MIX
Paper
FSC® C018306

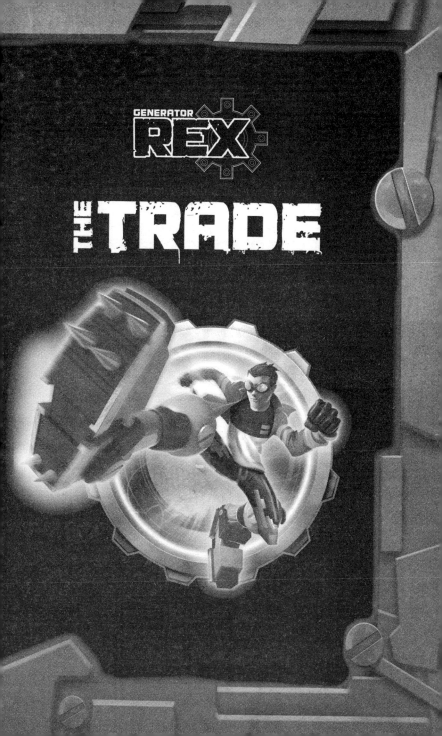

CHAPTER 1

FLUUUB!

HIGH ON A GRASSY VERGE in San Francisco's Golden Gate Park, something was growing. It was a man. At least, it *had* been.

His arms and legs were swelling, puffing up until they were several times their normal width. His whole body bulged, growing larger and more bloated with every second that passed.

Other park visitors began to scream and wail and run for their lives, as the man's skin became slick and gloopy and his limbs were drawn into his now bus-sized body.

Inside him, microscopic machines called nanites were altering his molecular structure, turning him from a human being into something new.

And into something *revolting*.

Rex yawned. He was curled up on a chair inside a Providence tank, wishing he were still in bed.

'Eight a.m.?' he groaned. 'Seriously? Who goes to the park at eight a.m.?'

Over by the door, Agent Six jabbed a series of buttons. 'Half of San Francisco,' he snapped, 'so we need to keep civilian casualties to a minimum.' He turned and glared at Rex through his sunglasses. 'Which means I need you awake.'

'I'm awake!' Rex protested. He stood up, stretched, then yawned again. 'But seriously – *eight a.m.*? Someone needs to teach these Evos how to tell time.'

Agent Six flicked a final switch and the door slid open. The sound of screaming and gunfire immediately filled the inside of the tank. Six stepped aside. 'Be my guest,' he said, motioning for Rex to lead the way.

'Ew,' Rex winced as he stepped down from the tank, 'what stinks?' He looked up and spotted the giant slug-like monster squirming on the grass just twenty or so metres away. 'Oh. Yeah. Forget I asked.'

Gunfire roared around them as a squadron of Providence Agents opened fire on the Evo. The Agents' bullets passed through the creature's jelly-like body, before emerging harmlessly on the other side.

A woman in a white lab coat stormed out from within the tank. 'Tell them to stop shooting,' Dr Holiday barked. 'That thing's unstable. Hit it in the wrong place and it pops like a balloon, then everyone here gets covered in nanite soup.'

Six raised an arm. The sound of gunfire immediately stopped.

Dr Holiday sighed with relief. '*Thank* you.'

'Looks like it's all down to you, kid,' said Six.

'So, what's new?' Rex asked. 'Anything special I need to know?'

'Don't get killed.'

'Thanks,' replied Rex. 'I'll bear that in mind.'

With a *whirr* and a *clank*, he put the nanites within his own body into action. Two enormous robotic fists grew from Rex's arms. He clanked them together a couple of times, testing them, then ran closer to the wriggling slug-beast.

'Hey, Gloopy,' Rex cried. He pointed to a small "KEEP OFF THE GRASS" sign sticking out of the ground. 'Can't you read?'

BEEEUUUK!

The Evo's mouth opened and a spray of bright

green gunk erupted from inside it. The gunk hit the sign, turning it into a sizzling pile of goo.

'OK,' Rex said, 'I'm going to take that as a "no".'

Raising a metal fist, Rex charged. One good, solid punch should be enough to knock the Evo out, he reckoned. After that, the rest would be easy.

Halfway there, Dr Holiday's voice crackled in his ear. 'Pop like a balloon, *remember*?'

'What? You mean I can't even – Whoa!'

Another spray of green slime spewed at him. His robotic arms retracted back into his body and a pair of jet turbines extended from his shoulders. With a *roar*, the Boogie Pack lifted into the air just as the grass at his feet dissolved in a puddle of sludge.

'So, we can't shoot it *or* hit it?' Rex asked, climbing higher above the park.

Dr Holiday's voice buzzed in his ear. 'No. We can't risk it spreading more nanites.'

Rex looked down. The slug Evo was squelching across the grass towards the Providence soldiers.

'I'd say reasoning with it is out of the question, too,' Rex muttered. He took a deep breath. 'Guess I'm just going to have to get my hands dirty.'

WHOOSH!

Rex rocketed towards the Evo, his face fixed in a mask of determination. This was going to get nasty!

As he passed above the slug-beast, he folded the jetpack back into his body. Almost at once he began to fall. Only the gloopy hide of the Evo stopped him hitting the ground.

Mechanical feet grew from Rex's legs, allowing him to grip onto the Evo's back, like a cowboy on a bucking bronco. The Evo growled as Rex pressed his hands against the monster's slimy skin.

'Trust me,' he grimaced, 'I don't like this any more than you do.'

Concentrating hard, Rex absorbed the nanites from inside the Evo. He felt them flow into his body, and as they did, the slug-creature became a slug-man, and then, finally, just a man.

Standing up, Rex wiped his sticky hands on the front of his trousers. 'Another one bites the ... um ... slime.'

Retracting his Punk Buster legs back into his body, Rex turned to find Agent Six standing in front of him. He was about to speak when the Punk Busters emerged again all on their own. 'Whoa, where'd they come from?' he frowned.

Agent Six raised an eyebrow. 'Everything OK?'

'Yeah, it's just –'

The legs pulled back into Rex's body. He paused for a moment, making sure they were gone for good this time. 'Weird,' he began, but a sudden *clanking* sound stopped him. The Punk Busters reformed yet again, only this time it was clear that something was very wrong.

Rex stared at his arms, which now had a huge pair of mechanical feet attached to the end of them. 'OK,' he swallowed. 'This is *not* good.'

CHAPTER 2

AGENT SIX STARED long and hard at the feet on the end of Rex's arms. 'Quit fooling around,' he said, at last.

Rex shook his head. 'Um ... I'm not doing this!'

The last word came out as a loud gasp, as the Punk Busters vanished without warning. Rex and Agent Six stood in silence for a few moments. Around them, the Providence Agents were dealing with the crowds and finding a blanket for the man who had, until very recently, been a slug.

'Well done, Rex,' said Dr Holiday, strolling across the grass to join them. 'That was some quick ...' She spotted their expressions. 'Those are worried faces,' she said. 'Why are we doing worried faces?'

With a metallic *clang*, just one of Rex's Smackhands emerged. Surprisingly, it chose to emerge from the top of his head. Rex looked up. 'I'm officially upgrading my "worried face" to a "terrified face",' he announced, quietly.

Dr Holiday blinked. 'That's ... unexpected,' she said.

'You sure you aren't doing this on purpose?' asked Agent Six, his eyes narrowing.

'I've got a fist growing out of my head!' Rex cried. 'Why would I do that on *purpose*?'

There was another sound of moving metal and his head returned to normal. Rex felt a brief moment of relief, before his Boogie Pack generated from his shoulders. He barely had time to realise what was happening before the jet turbines activated, launching him straight up into the air.

Down on the ground, Six and Holiday watched him streak towards the clouds. From that distance, they could barely even hear his panicked screams.

'OK,' Six said. 'I guess we'd better haul him in for testing.'

Dr Holiday nodded her head. 'I guess we should find a way to catch him first. Any suggestions?'

THUD!

Rex slammed down onto the grass. He had metal arms where his feet should be. He groaned loudly as he tried to sit up.

Six nodded. 'One or two.' He turned and pointed towards the closest Agent. 'Bring me a stretcher,' he ordered. 'And make it the strongest one we've got.'

Three hours later, Rex lay on an uncomfortable bed back at Providence headquarters. In the last one-hundred-and-eighty minutes he had been poked, prodded, jabbed, pierced, punctured, tickled, scratched and – briefly – electrocuted. It had not been his favourite morning.

'Nothing,' said Dr Holiday, shrugging.

Agent Six frowned. 'Nothing?'

'Nothing. He's absolutely fine.'

'Does that mean you'll stop sticking pins in me?' Rex asked, hopefully. Six ignored him.

'That's good news. He can get back on duty.'

'I'm not so sure that's a good idea,' Holiday argued.

'Why? You just said he was fine.'

'Because I really didn't enjoy the pins,' Rex continued. 'Or the electric shock.'

'The tests say he's fine,' Dr Holiday nodded, 'but we both know he *isn't* fine.'

'Wasn't really a fan of any of it, actually,' added Rex.

'We both saw what happened,' Holiday continued. She looked into Six's eyes, but all she saw was her reflection in his mirrored sunglasses. 'Something was seriously wrong.'

'*Was* seriously wrong,' Six said. 'Past tense. You just said it yourself, he's testing normal now.'

'I'd like to do some more tests,' Holiday told him. 'Central nervous system, higher brain function ...'

In one single bound, Rex leapt up from the bed. He stood beside them, back straight, trying to look as fit and healthy as possible. 'Tests?' he asked. 'No tests. Tests done. I'm fine, look.'

He stepped back and quickly cycled through his transformations. The Punk Buster feet appeared, only to vanish again a moment later. With a twitch of his shoulders, he brought out the Boogie Pack.

'Huh?' he grinned, turning left and right to show the jetpack off. 'Looking good, right?'

There was another metallic *whirr* and the jetpack disappeared. Raising his arms, Rex produced his Smackhands. He gave Six and Holiday a mechanical thumbs-up and flashed them a hopeful smile. 'See? Good as new. No more tests needed. Especially not ones that involve sticking pins in my face.'

Six stared at him, impassively. Eventually, he turned to Dr Holiday. 'What do you think?'

'You know what I think,' she replied.

'We'll keep an eye on him,' Six said. 'First sign of malfunction and I pull him back in, but for now he's back on duty.'

'All *right!*' Rex cheered, and then he jumped as the piercing scream of an alarm echoed around Providence HQ.

CHAPTER 3

REX AND AGENT SIX stood by the open back door of a Providence aircraft as it swooped low over a city.

'San Jose, California,' Six said. 'Tenth largest city in the United States. Population one million.'

Rex pointed. 'One million and one, if you count that guy twice.'

Below them, a two-headed Evo was stomping along a deserted street, tearing through cars with its long, clawed fingers. Both heads looked up at the sound of the aircraft's engine.

'Evasive action!' Six bellowed, as the Evo tore a street light from the concrete and hurled it like a javelin towards them. The boat-like aircraft banked sharply left and the metal pole soared harmlessly by.

But the sudden sideways movement sent Rex stumbling through the open door. 'Great,' he muttered, as he plunged towards the ground. 'Just great.'

The wind whistled around Rex, whipping at him

as he fell. Down below, the two-headed Evo bared twin sets of pointed teeth and let out a roar.

KA-BOOM!

A pair of enormous metal feet crunched down onto the street, shattering the concrete. Rex cracked his knuckles. 'It's punkin' time!' he grinned, swinging his leg just as the Evo hurled itself at him.

The tip of his metal foot caught the Evo under one of its chins. The monster staggered backwards, growling. Its four eyes narrowed, its claws splayed wide and it lunged once again.

It was bigger than Rex – much bigger – but it could move fast when it wanted to. Rex barely had time to raise a mechanical knee before the Evo was on him. There was a *crunch* as the knee was driven into the Evo's stomach, and both heads hissed loudly.

But still the monster kept coming. Rex saw the deadly claws swishing towards his face. Raising his arms, he brought out his Smackhands. The Evo growled with frustration when it found its attack blocked.

Pushing the Evo back, Rex fired a powerful uppercut against one of its jaws. With a squelchy *rrrip*, the head flew off. It bounced twice on the road, then skidded to a stop.

Rex looked down at the head. The head looked back. 'Um ... Oops,' he said. He turned to the head that was still attached to the body and smiled apologetically. 'We can probably just pack that in ice. I bet they can stitch it right back on.'

There was a sound like an enormous bubble popping, and another head emerged from within the Evo's shoulder. 'Or, you know, you could do *that*,' Rex said with a shudder.

Down on the ground, the severed head was already withering to dust. Up on the monster's shoulders, the other heads twisted their faces in rage.

'Nice Evo,' Rex said, stepping backwards. 'Good Evo.'

The creature began to advance. As it did, two large, bone-like blades grew from its forearms, stretching out until they almost touched the ground.

Rex smiled, nervously. 'Look, can't we just talk about this?'

SWISH!

One of the blades sliced through the air. Rex

ducked and rolled, just avoiding being sliced in two.

When Rex leapt back to his feet, his Smackhands were gone. In their place was the enormous blade of the Big Freakin' Sword. The blade's orange metal glinted in the sunlight.

'Not the talkative type, huh?' Rex asked. 'Well, it's your loss.'

He swung his sword-arm around in a wide arc. The Evo raised its twin blades, only to see them be chopped cleanly in half. The bones shattered as they hit the ground.

'Hey,' Rex smirked. 'I did warn you.'

Screeching, the Evo lunged once more, but Rex was ready. The butt of the sword crunched against one head, then the other. With a low groan, the monster sunk to its knees, then fell, faces first, to the ground.

'About time,' said Six, who was suddenly standing right behind Rex. 'Now do your thing so we can get out of here.'

'What? No "good work"?' grumbled Rex. The Big Freakin' Sword retracted back into his arm. 'No "congratulations on a job well done"?'

Six tried not to smile, but a twitch at the corner

of his mouth gave him away. 'Good work,' he said. 'Now fix him up and let's get back to the Keep.

'OK, OK,' Rex sighed. 'But what's the rush? The sun's shining, the sky's clear. I'm sure we flew over a beach about thirty miles back. We could swing back there and —'

'We're on a mission, not a day trip,' Six reminded him. 'But ... we'll see. For now, though, get curing.'

Rex grinned. Six could be pretty stern, but he did have a sense of fun buried deep inside his designer suit. A trip to the beach was just what Rex needed to forget about the pins-in-the-face experience.

But first things first. Pressing his hands against the unconscious Evo's heads, Rex felt the nanites flooding into him. In moments, the figure on the ground began to change. The claws became more like fingers. The extra head slowly sunk back towards the shoulder. The transformation was halfway complete when things started to go wrong.

'Not again!' Rex cried. His Smackhands had appeared where his feet should have been. He wobbled unsteadily, then both legs slid in opposite directions and he thudded down onto the road.

There was the sound of machinery moving and the Punk Buster legs wrapped around his arms. Rex stared down at his limbs. He'd never been able to call up the Smackhands and Punk Busters at the same time before, but now here they all were. Just in completely the wrong places.

Agent Six touched the communication device in his ear. 'Evac team,' he barked. 'Rex is in trouble and we've got an Evo stuck mid-transformation. Clean up needed. *Now.*'

'What's happening?' Rex gasped. The machines suddenly felt tight on his arms and legs. 'It ... it hurts.'

'In that case, you can thank me for this later,' said Six. He summoned an Agent to his side and, with a brisk nod, took from him an extremely long needle. Six flicked the anaesthetic inside the needle and before Rex could protest, slipped the point into what was left of Rex's right arm.

For a moment, Rex saw the world go fuzzy at the edges, and then everything slowly faded to black.

CHAPTER 4

'**I** KNEW IT WAS A BAD idea letting him out,' Dr Holiday said. Rex was lying on another hospital-type bed. He was more or less back to normal, aside from the bruise on his upper arm where Six had poked the needle into him. A number of machines were connected to him by thin wires. Every few seconds, one of the machines would go *bleep*.

Dr Holiday shook her head angrily. 'He should never have gone out. He needed more tests.'

'More tests,' Rex groaned. '*Yay*.'

'What, would you rather go through all that again?' Holiday snapped. 'Your transformations going out of control every time you use them?'

'Well, no, but –'

'Anything could've happened to you out there, Rex,' she continued. 'You could've been badly hurt. Or worse.'

Rex shrugged. 'I know, it's just ... do you *have* to stick more pins in my face?'

Dr Holiday rolled her eyes. 'I stuck *one* pin in your face *one* time to test for nerve damage. *One.*'

'It felt like more,' Rex muttered. 'Anyway, one pin in your face is one too many, that's what I always say.'

'No more pins, Rex, I promise,' Holiday said. She glared pointedly at Agent Six. 'But maybe I'll be allowed to finish the other tests this time, so we can figure out what's happening to you.'

Agent Six turned to Holiday. 'I understand you were unhappy with us taking him out,' he said, 'but the mission required Rex's input.'

'The *mission*?' Holiday spluttered. 'What about Rex? Did you stop to think what *he* "required"?'

A frosty silence hung in the air for a few moments. Finally, Six asked: 'What have you found out?'

Dr Holiday gave a sigh. 'Nothing. Well, not much.' She handed Agent Six a bundle of paper. Numbers and symbols covered the pages. 'I've been monitoring him since you brought him back in. These are the readings.'

'They're all over the place,' Six frowned.

'You can say that again. Now turn to the back pages.'

Agent Six flipped through the bundle. 'Normal,' he said.

'They levelled off quickly,' Holiday nodded. 'Holding steady now.'

'So, what you're saying is, he's fine?' said Six.

'Look at those charts!' Holiday said. 'He's normal for now, but he's far from "fine". Whatever happened to him out there could happen again.'

'*Could* happen again,' said Six. '*Could*.'

While Six and Holiday were arguing, Rex quietly slipped down from the bed. Carefully, he peeled back the tape holding the wires against his body. He had almost removed them all when one of the medical machines began to beep loudly.

'Back on the bed, mister,' Holiday told him. She gave him a stern look. 'I'm not done with you yet.'

Agent Six and the doctor watched him until he had reattached every one of the wires and climbed back up onto the bed. 'Hey,' he said, 'worth a try, right?'

'Nanite overload,' said Six, quietly.

'Excuse me?' asked Holiday.

'Nanite overload,' Six said again. 'Happened before, remember? Too many nanites. Sent his whole system crazy.'

'I remember,' Rex nodded. 'My face was a sack of metal pus. That's not something you forget in a hurry. But this isn't like that.'

Holiday nodded. 'He's right,' she said. 'This is different. The readings are nothing like they were then. Something else is causing Rex's ... problems.'

'What then?' Six asked.

'I wish I knew. I'm going to have to run –'

'More tests,' groaned Rex, finishing her sentence for her. 'OK then, Doc, do whatever you have to do.' He glared at Agent Six. 'But do not even think about coming near my face with anything sharp.'

'White Knight wants him match-fit in two hours,' said Six, ignoring Rex and talking instead to Dr Holiday. White Knight was Agent Six's boss, and the leader of the Providence organisation.

'Two hours?' Holiday yelped. 'That's nowhere near enough time. We need to keep him out of action until we've figured out exactly what's going on. No matter how long it takes.'

'I can't see White Knight agreeing to that,' Six said. He met Holiday's eye and gave a curt nod of his head.

'But I'll see if I can buy you some more time, at least.'

The others watched him leave the lab. Once he was gone, Dr Holiday turned to Rex. 'Now,' she said, picking up a long syringe with an even longer needle on the end, 'don't worry, this isn't going to hurt.'

CHAPTER 5

REX WAS BORED.

He was in his own room, lying on his own bed, flicking through the channels on the TV. There was nothing on but soaps and makeover shows. He jabbed a button on the remote and clicked through another half dozen channels, each one more terrible than the last.

With a final press of the remote control, the TV screen went dark. Rex lay back on the bed, his hands behind his head. He was bored. Really bored.

Bored.

Bored.

Bored.

It wouldn't have been so bad if Bobo or Noah had been around. His friends were always good company, even if one of them *was* a talking chimp. Even Agent Six would be *someone* to talk to, but Dr Holiday had made it clear that Rex had to be kept in isolation. 'For observation,' she'd said.

Rex looked over at the CCTV cameras mounted

in the corners of the room, watching his every move. Still, at least they weren't being secretive about it – the cameras were almost impossible to miss.

Swinging his legs down onto the floor, Rex turned to the closest camera and waved. 'Hey, Doc,' he said. 'How long did you say I have to stay in here?'

Dr Holiday's face appeared on a screen on the wall. 'Twenty-four hours,' she said. 'That's all.'

Rex nodded. 'Right. And how long have I been here for?'

Dr Holiday looked at her watch. 'Eleven minutes,' she told him.

'*Eleven minutes*,' Rex groaned. 'Seriously?'

'It'll be over in no time,' Holiday smiled. 'Why don't you watch some TV to take your mind off it?'

'I already tried that.'

On screen, Holiday shrugged. 'Try again.' With that, the screen went dark.

'Try again,' Rex muttered. He picked up the remote and switched the television on again. A glamorous soap opera actress sobbed hysterically in close up.

Click. He changed channel. A bearded man was planting seeds in a garden.

Click. A middle-aged woman was having her hair done by a man in a yellow shirt.

Click. A scorpion-like Evo was smashing police cars with its deadly tail.

Click. A man in dungarees was painting the outside of a house.

Rex blinked. *Wait.* He clicked back a channel and the scorpion Evo filled the screen again. A news reporter's voice was explaining that the monster had appeared from nowhere, and had already destroyed half a city block. The text at the bottom of the screen identified the location as "Fremont, California".

Rex turned back to the CCTV camera. 'Uh, Doc,' he began, 'are you seeing this?'

There was a pause as the camera moved to take in what was happening on the TV. Dr Holiday's face appeared on the wall-mounted screen again. 'I see it,' she said, 'but it's not your problem.'

The door to Rex's room opened with a *swish*. 'On the contrary,' said Agent Six, looming in the doorway. 'It's very much his problem.'

Rex stood in the Providence aircraft hangar, listening to Dr Holiday and Agent Six argue. He had been standing there listening to them for almost ten minutes now, and they still didn't seem any closer to reaching an agreement.

'You can't take him out,' Dr Holiday snapped. 'Anything could happen.'

'I've done all I can,' Six replied. 'White Knight wants him out in the field. His readings are still fine. Chances are it was a temporary glitch.'

'And chances are it might not have been!'

Rex whistled quietly. He nodded to a group of Providence Agents, who were boarding the aircraft beside them.

'We've got an out-of-control Evo tearing up the city,' Six said.

'And you've got a hundred Agents and a dozen tanks already at the scene,' said Holiday. 'You don't need Rex.'

'Correction. We've now got seventeen Agents and two tanks. The Evo took care of the rest.' He touched a finger to his ear, listening to a voice on his communicator. 'Make that one tank.'

'Not my problem,' said Holiday. 'I can't let you take him.'

'And I can't let him stay,' Six replied.

'Rex,' they both said at once, 'come with me.'

Rex held up his hands. 'Look, guys, it's nice to be wanted and everything, but –'

A viewing screen on the wall beside them blinked into life. The ghostly pale face of White Knight appeared. 'What's the hold up?' he demanded, gruffly.

'Six is trying to take Rex out on a mission,' Dr Holiday said, hurriedly.

White Knight nodded. 'I know. I gave the order.'

'Sir, I really have to object! I don't think –'

'Objection noted,' said White Knight. 'But he's going.'

Dr Holiday opened her mouth to say something else, but Agent Six jumped in first. 'I'll bring him back in one piece,' he said, taking Rex by the arm and steering him towards the aircraft's entrance. 'Well ... two at the most.'

'Was that a joke, Six?' Rex asked, grinning broadly. 'You hear that, Doc? Six made a joke.'

Agent Six flashed him a serious look.

'Um ... that *was* a joke, right?' asked Rex, suddenly nervous. 'Right, Six?'

The door to the aircraft slid closed. Dr Holiday could only watch as the vehicle blasted off, leaving her all alone in the empty hangar.

'Good luck,' she said, quietly. Somehow, she had a feeling Rex was going to need it.

CHAPTER 6

ON A DESERTED STREET in Fremont, California, twelve tanks smouldered quietly. The semi-conscious bodies of almost a hundred Agents lay scattered across the tarmac, groaning and whimpering in pain.

Smoke poured from within shattered store fronts. Cars lay upturned, their metal frames shredded, their windscreens shattered. Somewhere in the wreckage, a police siren wailed once, then slowed to a stop.

In the middle of the street was a hole. It was wide and deep, easily large enough to fit one of the broken Providence tanks. Down in the hole, the scorpion Evo lurked.

'Now there's something you don't see every day,' Rex whispered, ducking low behind the smoking remains of a pizza delivery van. He gasped, sharply. 'Whoa!' Beside him, Agent Six went tense.

'What's wrong?' he hissed.

'Pepperoni,' said Rex, happily. He reached in

through the broken doors of the van and pulled out a cheese-coated triangle of pizza. 'Want a slice?'

Steel flashed before Rex's eyes and the pizza left his hand. He looked up to find the slice stuck to the end of one of Six's swords. With a flick, Six sent the pizza hurtling across the street. Rex watched it splatter messily against a wall.

'Hey, I was going to eat that!'

'Junk food later,' Six growled. 'Fight Evo *now*.'

'OK, OK,' Rex sighed. 'But when we're finished here, you owe me a twelve-inch deep pan.'

'Deal,' Six said.

'With *extra cheese*.'

'Don't push your luck –'

KER-ASSSH!

A curved stinger, larger than Rex's head, tore through the side of the van. Rex and Six jumped back as the van was lifted into the air. The scorpion Evo hissed at them, angrily.

'Hi there,' said Rex, brightly. 'I don't suppose you'd like to surrender quietly?'

The scorpion's tail snapped down. Rex was knocked sideways by Agent Six, just as the van smashed down onto the road. Six growled in pain as part of the axle slammed down onto his legs, pinning them against the ground.

'You OK?' Rex asked, reaching down to help Six.

'Fine. Forget me,' Six barked. He tried to pull his legs free, but they were held fast. 'Stop *that* thing.'

Rex nodded. 'You're the boss, boss.' He stood up. The scorpion-creature was larger than the pizza van had been, even before it was smashed to pieces. It had four yellow eyes, each one the size of a football. The eyes were fixed on the helpless Six. Rex knew he had to lead the Evo away.

'Didn't anyone tell you it's rude to stare?' Rex said, stepping between the Evo and Agent Six. He raised both arms, extended the index fingers, then poked the scorpion in two of its eyes. The Evo howled with rage.

'You want me?' Rex cried. He ran past the scorpion. 'Then come get me!'

Rex powered forward, leaping over fallen Agents and sliding across the bonnets of abandoned cars. Behind him, he heard the *tick, tick, tick* of the scorpion's legs as it raced after him across the concrete. With every step, the sound became louder. The Evo was gaining, and it was gaining fast.

'So, you can run,' Rex muttered. 'But let's see if you can outrun the Rex Ride!'

Rex leapt into the air. As he did, an orange and silver hover-bike formed beneath him. The street became a blur around him as he opened the throttle and sent the bike hurtling along the street.

Tick, tick, tick.

Tick, tick, tick.

Rex looked back over his shoulder. He could barely believe what he saw. The scorpion Evo was still gaining steadily, its pincer-legs carrying it along at incredible speed.

'OK, so you *can* outrun the Rex Ride,' Rex said. He suddenly didn't feel as confident as he had a moment ago. 'But what if I – Ack!'

The hover-bike vanished. Still racing forward at breakneck speed, Rex clattered onto the ground, bounced twice, then rolled to a clumsy stop. Winded, he clambered back to his feet. A trickle of blood ran down his cheek, from a cut on his forehead. He ignored it, and focused instead on the enormous scorpion-monster teetering towards him.

'That's it, big guy,' he spat. 'Let's see how you like the Slam Cannon.'

Rex waited. Nothing happened. The Evo hurried closer.

'The *Slam Cannon*,' Rex said again.

Again, nothing.

'Aw, man,' Rex groaned, before a swiping blow from the scorpion's tail sent him tumbling across the tarmac. A pain, like none he'd ever felt before, suddenly burned through his whole body, but it was nothing to do with the Evo's attack. Something was happening to him. Something bad.

A scream burst from Rex's lips. His back arched and his muscles bunched into knots. A deafening *clanking* and *whirring* of machinery rose up, as his transformations began to activate one after another.

Smackhands, Punk Busters, Boogie Pack; they appeared one after another, vanishing as quickly as they had come. The Slam Cannon appeared next, forming around his shoulder even as the Rex Ride formed around his feet.

'Wh-what's happening?' Rex cried, as the Big Freakin' Sword appeared briefly at the end of one arm, and then the other. There was a loud grinding of metal as the Punk Buster feet appeared and fought for space with the Rex Ride. The arm without the sword attached became a Smackhand. Through the pain, Rex realised that every one of his transformations was happening at the same time!

Even the Evo had hesitated, confused by what was happening to the boy on the ground. Deep inside its deranged brain, though, it came to the conclusion that it really couldn't care less. The boy had attacked it, and for that, the boy would die.

Raising its lethal stinger, the scorpion fixed its four eyes on Rex, and crept slowly forward.

CHAPTER 7

'GET UP, REX. Get up!'

Back at Providence HQ, Dr Holiday was watching events through a CCTV camera mounted on one of the battle-damaged tanks. She had seen Six trapped by the pizza van and Rex's machines begin to malfunction. More importantly, she could now see the monstrous Evo stalking towards Rex, who was now thrashing around in pain.

Another screen blinked into life beside her. Dr Holiday turned and came face to face with a video image of White Knight.

'This is all *your* fault,' she told him, forgetting for a moment who she was talking to. 'I told you he wasn't ready. I told you it wasn't safe!'

'Rex was vital to this mission,' White Knight said.

Dr Holiday threw up her arms. 'The mission,' she cried, 'it's always about the mission!'

'Yes,' said White Knight, flatly. 'It's always about the mission.'

Holiday folded her arms across her chest.

'Then maybe we're on the wrong mission,' she muttered, and she turned back to the main screen.

Rex's teeth were clamped tightly together. Veins bulged in his neck until they stood out like blue ropes from his skin. Just a few metres away, the scorpion Evo drew back its tail and prepared to strike.

CLANG!

A pair of katana swords blocked the scorpion's attack. Its four eyes swivelled to find Agent Six staring back at it. 'You messed up my suit,' Six said. 'No one messes up my suit.'

The tail pulled back, then stabbed sharply towards the centre of Six's chest. Six stepped sideways and swished the swords down. The scorpion's stinger *clacked* hard against the pavement. 'Clearly you weren't listening,' Six said. '*No one* messes up my suit.'

Six brought a knee up to his chest, then fired a devastating kick against one of the scorpion's front legs. The armoured limb buckled and the Evo stumbled sideways, screeching in pain.

On the ground, Rex was doing more or less the same thing. He cried out in agony as his transformations continued to switch back and forth, there one minute, gone the next.

'His biometric signs are failing,' crackled a voice in Agent Six's ear. It was Dr Holiday, speaking to him via the communicator. 'You have to get him out of there *now*.'

'Kind of in the middle of something here,' grunted Six. He ducked another swipe of the scorpion's tail.

'*I don't care*,' Holiday snarled. 'Get Rex and ...'

There was a hiss of static, and then another voice broke in. 'Subdue the Evo,' ordered White Knight. 'Then you can help Rex.'

'Yes, sir,' Six said. He twirled his swords in front of the Evo, beckoning it closer. 'Let's get this over with.'

The scorpion raised its two front legs. Six swung both swords around in a wide arc. The Evo squealed as both its legs flopped down onto the street.

'That was for the suit,' Six said, before a movement down near his feet caught his eye.

From inside the severed limbs, hundreds of smaller

scorpion-creatures were emerging. They weren't much larger than normal scorpions, but they moved at incredible speed.

Six stepped back as the scorpions swarmed towards him. He *swooshed* his sword down at the ground. Sparks flashed as the blades hit the concrete road surface and five, ten, twenty of the little creatures were sliced in half.

But still they kept coming. For every one Six killed, a dozen more emerged from inside the severed limbs. They were pouring from the stumps on the Evo's body, too, where the legs had been attached. In moments, the road around Six was a heaving mass of legs and bodies and little curved tails.

Six raised a foot and slammed it down on the closest scorpion. It exploded in a spray of green goop. He looked up and met the gaze of the larger creature. 'And now you've gone and messed up my shoes.' Six raised his swords again. 'Ugly, this just isn't your day.'

Back at Providence HQ, Dr Holiday was ranting at a viewing screen. White Knight's face filled the screen. He did not look happy.

'The Evo isn't important,' she said. 'Saving Rex *is*. He could die.'

'And if we let the Evo go, it could kill hundreds,' White Knight replied. 'Better to contain it now than risk a major incident.'

'We've already got a major incident!' Holiday protested. 'Rex is undergoing some kind of ... of ... *mutation*. The nanites are doing something to him, and I don't know what it is!'

'And I'm confident in your ability to find out, Doctor,' White Knight said, 'just as soon as we've stopped the Evo.'

'Let the other Agents handle the Evo! Isn't that what they're paid for?'

Dr Holiday turned and snatched up the communicator. 'Six, let the other Agents fight that thing. Concentrate on saving Rex!'

'Ignore that, Agent Six,' White Knight instructed. 'Your orders stand. Neutralise that Evo!'

Meanwhile, in Fremont, Agent Six was trying to do just that. He sat on the scorpion's back, one arm wrapped around its tail, the other pulling on its armoured head. Only a few of the smaller scorpion-creatures remained. They scuttled and scurried over the crushed remains of their brothers and sisters, wondering how many of them could have been wiped out by just one pair of feet.

A few metres away, Rex's whole body spasmed, then went limp as he finally fell unconscious. Neither he, nor Agent Six, noticed the black armoured car creeping along the street. They didn't notice it rolling to a stop right beside Rex, or the passenger door slowly easing open.

And they didn't notice the hulking Evo arms reaching out and dragging Rex inside.

CHAPTER 8

SIX LOOKED UP AT the sound of the car door slamming closed. He realised immediately what had happened. If he released his grip on the Evo now, though, it would either kill him, escape, or both.

'Stop that car!' he bellowed, to anyone within earshot. Fifteen Providence Agents crept out from hiding places and stood in front of the approaching car, blocking its path.

The car did not slow.

'Open fire!' one of the Agents cried. In unison, they all hoisted their machine-guns to their shoulders and sprayed bullets at the oncoming vehicle.

The car did not slow. Fourteen Agents dived sideways out of harm's way. One wasn't so lucky. The car hit him and he was tossed up onto the bonnet. He clung on tightly for a few moments, before the car screeched around the corner and the Agent rolled sideways and hit the ground with an '*Oof!*'

Up on the Evo's back, Agent Six cursed. Dr Holiday would *never* let him hear the end of this. Twisting at the waist, he fired a kick against the back of the scorpion-monster's head. It hissed softly through its mouth, like the sound of a balloon slowly deflating, and then it collapsed, unconscious, onto the pavement.

'Evo down,' Six said into the communicator.

'About time,' Dr Holiday replied. 'How's Rex? We lost the video feed.'

Six took a deep breath. 'It's funny you should ask.'

'You lost him?'

Six shook his head and wiped a smear of squished scorpion slime from the front of his suit. 'No, I didn't lose him. He was taken. Big difference.'

Dr Holiday stepped closer, until her nose was almost touching Six's. Her face was red with rage. 'He was *taken* because you weren't watching him!' she said.

'I wasn't watching him because I was wrestling an arachnid the size of a bus,' Six replied. 'You'd be amazed how that sort of thing can hold your attention.'

'This isn't funny, Six,' Holiday said. She chewed on her lip and wrung her hands together. 'Anyone could've taken him, and anything could've happened. He's all alone out there. Defenceless.'

For a few moments, Six didn't speak. Eventually, he gave a brief nod of his head. 'What can I do to help?'

Holiday turned her back on him and made for the door. 'You can stay out of my way,' she said. 'And if you see White Knight, tell him the same thing.'

She left the room, closing the door with a *slam* that shook the walls. Agent Six raised one neat eyebrow. 'Well,' he said to himself, 'that went about as well as could be expected.'

Half an hour later, Dr Holiday was in her lab. Spread out on the table in front of her were all the printouts of Rex's biometric readings taken when his transformations were going haywire. She had scribbled notes on over half of the pages, as she'd tried to figure out what the readings meant.

On a video screen beside her, the CCTV footage

of Rex's battle with the scorpion Evo was playing on a loop. It showed everything, right up until the point half a dozen of the mini-scorpions crawled over the camera lens. The feed had gone dead almost right away after that.

There was a soft knock at the lab door. Holiday didn't look up from the printouts. 'Come in,' she instructed, and the door was opened.

'Hi, Dr Holiday. You wanted to see me?'

'Noah, good, you're here,' said Holiday. She smiled at the blond-haired teen as he entered the room. 'I need your help. Rex is in trouble.'

'Why am I not surprised?' Noah asked. 'What's up this time?'

'I'm not sure,' Holiday admitted. 'I think he was losing control of his nanites, but I can't say for certain.'

'Can't you just run some tests or whatever? Isn't that how it normally works?'

'I could. If I knew where he was,' Dr Holiday said. 'He's been abducted.'

'*Abducted?*' gasped Noah, his eyes widening. 'By who?'

'That's what we're going to try to find out,' she

replied. 'But first, we need to figure out what's causing him to lose control.'

Noah frowned. 'Right. And you wanted me here because ...?'

'Because I could use another pair of eyes,' Holiday said. She gestured down at the printouts. 'Take a look. Tell me what you see.'

Noah bent over the table and looked at each page in turn. After several minutes he straightened up. 'Numbers,' he said. 'Lots of them.'

'I was hoping for a little more than that.'

'You're the brains of the outfit, Dr Holiday,' Noah told her. 'Me? I'm just kind of ... moral support. If there's something out of place, you'll find it, not me.'

Dr Holiday's body went stiff. 'Wait,' she said, 'what did you say?'

Noah thought back. 'If there's something out of place –'

'Out of place,' she repeated, quietly. 'Out of place.'

Her fingers danced across the nearest computer keyboard. The screen changed to display a detailed map of California. 'The malfunctions only happened when Rex was out on a mission. Here, here and here.'

Three red dots appeared close together on the map, showing the locations of Rex's recent battles.

'They're all within fifty miles of one another,' Noah commented.

'Exactly! So what if something in that area was causing Rex's nanites to malfunction?'

Noah stared hard at the screen. 'Something like that?' he said, pointing to an area on the map.

Dr Holiday followed his finger. With a yelp of delight she jumped back from the monitor. 'Noah,' she cried, 'you are a *genius!*'

CHAPTER 9

DARKNESS SWAM BEHIND Rex's eyelids, and white noise poured into his ears like rushing sand. Beneath him, the floor seemed determined to shake him awake.

Gradually, the sound of sand faded and he was able to pick out other noises. The roaring of a car engine. The low muttering of a male voice. The unsteady crashing of his own heart.

But he was only vaguely aware of them all at best. They were background noise, nothing more. What he was much more aware of was the pain.

It spread out from the centre of his chest and coiled around his arms until it found the very tips of his fingers. It lay like a weight in his stomach and it burned at both of his legs. It throbbed behind his eyes, up over his head and down to the base of his skull. Every single part of him hurt, and the ⌐ awake he became, the worse the pain got.

A burst of pure agony explode⌐

and it suddenly became very heavy. A voice somewhere above him grunted. 'Watch out for his sword,' it said.

'It ripped through the seat,' another voice said.

'It'll rip through *you* if you're not careful,' said the first speaker. Rex thought he recognised the voice, but there was too much happening for him to worry about that now.

The Big Freakin' Sword retracted back into Rex's arm, but the pain didn't ease off. The darkness behind his eyes seemed to shimmer, and Rex realised, too late, that he was falling unconscious once again.

Some time passed. Rex couldn't even begin to guess how much. When he woke again, the floor still felt as if it were moving, and his body still hurt. He was able to open his eyes but he didn't, not yet. He had a feeling he was in danger, and opening his eyes meant he'd have to face that danger head-on. He wasn't ready for that.

He could feel straps across his arms and legs. He was lying flat, arms out to the side and slightly above his head, feet bound tightly together. In his half-awake brain, he imagined himself looking like a big letter Y.

The surface beneath him was vibrating, occasionally bouncing him around. He guessed he was travelling inside some sort of vehicle. Not Providence, though. They wouldn't tie him up, would they? *Actually*, he thought, *nothing would surprise me*.

He could sense other people around him, but he had no idea how many. They weren't talking, but he could feel them watching to see if he was awake.

Or were they? Was he just being paranoid? There was nothing else for it. He had to know. One way or another, he had to know.

Gently, like the fluttering of a butterfly's wings, Rex's eyes began to open. Light flooded in, forcing him to blink rapidly. His eyes had just begun to adjust to the brightness when a shadow passed over him.

Rex opened his eyes fully, just in time to see a massive fist come speeding towards his face.

'Lights out,' said the familiar voice. Rex's head thudded against the floor of the armoured car, and for the third time that day, he found himself slipping silently into unconsciousness.

CHAPTER 10

GENT SIX STOOD BEFORE a large viewing screen which was displaying a map of California. Beside him, a video screen blinked into life, showing White Knight's face. The Providence leader looked unhappy at having been disturbed.

'This had better be good, Doctor,' White Knight warned. 'I am an extremely busy man.'

Dr Holiday bit her tongue. 'I'll try not to keep you, *sir*,' she said. She crossed to the wall displaying the map. Noah was already there, standing to one side, looking slightly awkward.

Before Holiday could start to explain her findings, a door at the back of the room opened and Bobo strolled in. The chimp stretched, yawned, then adjusted his little red hat.

'What's up?' he asked. 'What'd I miss?'

'Listen up,' Six told him, not turning from the map. 'We're about to have it all spelled out.'

Bobo shuffled over to join the rest of the group.

Dr Holiday cleared her throat. 'I was looking over Rex's tests results, trying to figure out what was causing his machines to malfunction,' she began.

Bobo raised a hand. 'Uh ... malfunction?'

'Read the report,' Six said.

'Can't you just give me the highlights?' Bobo asked. Reading reports wasn't really his thing.

'Rex's machines malfunctioned. Rex got kidnapped. That's pretty much it,' said Noah.

'Thanks, kid,' said Bobo.

'No problem.'

'Can we get on with it?' barked White Knight.

Holiday nodded. 'As I said, I was trying to figure out the cause of the malfunctions, but was getting nowhere. By the time I got him back here, his tests were more or less normal. Well, normal for Rex, anyway.'

'We already know this,' said Agent Six. 'What's your point?'

Dr Holiday glared at him. 'I'm getting to my point,' she said, coldly. 'It was Noah who worked it out, really.'

'Worked what out?' Six asked.

Holiday pointed at the map. 'Worked out that

there wasn't anything wrong with Rex. There was something at the battle sites that was making his nanites act strangely.'

'That was why he was fine whenever you brought him back in,' Noah added.

Agent Six thought about this. 'OK, I'll bite,' he said, at last. 'What was causing the problems.'

'Map, zoom sector eight-alpha,' Dr Holiday said. On the wall behind her, the map zoomed in on a single area.

'What we looking at?' Bobo asked.

'Silicon Valley,' Dr Holiday announced.

Bobo looked more closely at the map. 'Don't look like no valley to me,' he said. 'It's all buildings and city blocks, far as I can see.'

'It *is* all buildings and city blocks,' Dr Holiday explained. 'Silicon Valley is home to some of the most high-tech companies in the world, producing some of the most advanced software and tech on the planet.'

'Oh, yeah,' Bobo shrugged. 'I knew that.'

'His nanites were sent into overload because of his proximity to some video game companies?' White Knight snorted. 'I don't buy it.'

'It's not just video game companies!' Holiday protested. 'There are hundreds of companies located there – factories developing nanite-powered computer chips, designers messing with tech they don't really know anything about.'

She gestured to the satellite map, and to the hundreds of buildings it showed. 'Who's to say what else is going on there?' Holiday asked. 'Anything could've interfered with Rex's control over his nanites.'

'It's ... possible, I suppose,' Agent Six admitted.

'Still not buying it,' said White Knight. 'You're clutching at straws, Dr Holiday. We need something concrete.'

'You want concrete?' Holiday asked. She tapped a few buttons on a computer keyboard and a large red blob appeared on the map. 'How's this for concrete?'

'What is it?' White Knight asked.

'Evo activity. Our scanners picked it up early this morning.'

'Who or what is it?' Six asked.

Holiday shrugged. 'Can't say,' she said. She looked meaningfully at White Knight. 'Too much *interference*.'

'Unusual Evo activity in an area of high-tech interference, close to where Rex started losing control,' Noah said. 'We're not clutching at straws, we're holding an iron bar. With both hands.'

Everyone turned to look at him. Noah spotted their puzzled expressions. 'Well, I know what I meant,' he muttered.

'It's the best lead we've got,' Dr Holiday said. 'It's our best chance of finding Rex.'

White Knight stayed silent.

'All I ask is that you send out Six and some Agents to check it out,' Holiday continued. 'Something's going on. Maybe they can find out what.'

'Request denied,' White Knight replied.

There was a moment of silence, broken only by the shocked gasp of Dr Holiday. '*Denied?*' she spluttered. 'You can't be serious!'

'I appreciate your concern, Doctor,' White Knight said. 'But with the amount of Evo activity going on of late, we're already fully stretched. I cannot spare anyone.'

'But ... *Rex* –'

'– can handle himself,' White Knight said.

'Normally, maybe,' Noah said. 'But if he's malfunctioning, who knows what might happen to him?'

'Do I really have to repeat myself?' White Knight said. 'Request *denied*.'

Dr Holiday slipped off her lab coat and let it fall to the floor. 'Fine,' she said. 'Then I quit.'

Agent Six raised an eyebrow. Even White Knight appeared surprised.

'And so do I,' said Noah, standing shoulder to shoulder with Dr Holiday.

Dr Holiday nodded. 'And so does Bobo.'

'You tell him, Toots,' Bobo nodded. 'Wait,' he added, quickly. 'I do?'

'So that's the choice you have, sir,' Dr Holiday said, staring directly at White Knight's face on the screen. 'Send out the Agents, or watch us walk out the door.'

She leaned down until her nose was almost touching the monitor. 'What's it to be?'

CHAPTER 11

REX OPENED HIS EYES and immediately wished that he hadn't.

The ceiling overhead spun and twirled like a fairground ride, making him feel sick. He closed his eyes again, shook his head, and took a deep breath.

When he opened his eyes for a second time, the room had stopped spinning. There was a large spotlight mounted on the ceiling, pointing directly down at him. The light was off, and he could see his reflection in the curved glass.

He was on a bed, like the one back in Dr Holiday's lab. He had no idea where he was, but one thing he did know – this definitely was *not* Providence base.

The room he was in was small and cramped. Paint peeled in large flakes from the walls and dust covered almost every surface. Machines and lab equipment stood all around the bed. Wires ran from the machines. Each wire was attached to some part of his body – his chest, his arms, his legs and his head.

In the corner of the room, a printer spewed out page after page of paper, each sheet covered with numbers and letters and strange, cryptic symbols. Rex was too far away to be able to read the pages properly. Even if he was closer, though, he doubted he'd make any sense of them.

Rex took another deep breath, then gave a short yelp of pain. His lungs ached. Now he came to think about it, *all* of him ached. He tried to think back to what had happened to him.

There had been an Evo, he remembered that. A nasty one with an even nastier tail. He searched his memories, but they were hazy, as if lost in a thick fog.

He'd been travelling fast, he thought. And then he'd been travelling slowly, and then he hadn't been travelling at all. Something had hit him. The Evo? The ground? He couldn't say for sure, and then ... And then ...

And then what? Darkness and pain, that was all that came back to him. Darkness and pain and ... a big letter Y?

He remembered! He'd been taken somewhere, strapped down, unable to move. Someone had punched him and knocked him out. Someone familiar.

Rex tried to sit up. The moment he moved, a machine somewhere near his right shoulder began to bleep. A LED display on the front of the machine flashed up "300 VOLTS" and a powerful electric shock surged through Rex's body.

'*Whoa*,' Rex hissed, when the shock had passed. 'That was harsh.'

He lay still for a moment, making sure he wasn't about to be zapped again. Finally, he raised his head, just a little. 'Hello?' he called. The door to the room was closed. It looked to be made of a thick metal. Rex hoped it wasn't sound proof. 'Hello? Anyone there?'

There was no reply from beyond the door. 'Great,' Rex mumbled. 'Just great.'

He craned his neck until he could see the machine that had zapped him. It was about the size of a car radio, with an enormous battery pack attached to the base. There were a few buttons and switches on the front, and two wires ran from the front. Rex followed the cables with his eyes. They ended somewhere on his chest, too high up for him to be able to see them.

Slowly, cautiously, he moved his hands up his

chest until he found the ends of the wires. They ran down inside the neck of his t-shirt, where they were attached to his skin by two circular stickers.

His fingers shook as he carefully began to pull the stickers away. Beside him, the LED display lit up.

"500 VOLTS".

BZZZZZT!

Rex's back arched and his limbs went stiff. He pulled his hands away from the wires and shot the machine an accusing look. 'Dude, *seriously!*' he said.

The machine was within arm's reach. It didn't zap him again when he positioned his hand beside it, fist clenched. 'You just earned yourself a taste of the B.F.S.,' he told it. He concentrated on making the sword appear.

The sword did *not* appear.

He tried again, trying to form his Smackhands this time. Once again, nothing happened. Something was suppressing his nanites. He was powerless!

'Could today get any worse?' he groaned.

BZZZZZZT!

He cried out in pain, then turned back to the machine. "900 VOLTS" was flashing on the display screen. 'Ow! What was *that* for?' he demanded, but the machine didn't answer.

Rex lay his head back on the bed and tried to figure out his next move. He couldn't transform. He couldn't attract anyone's attention. If he tried to sit up, he got electrocuted. He had to admit, things weren't looking good.

Sighing, he turned his head so he was looking at the machine again. That was his main problem right now. If he could just find a way to disable it, he'd have a fighting chance at escape.

But who was he kidding? The tech stuff was Dr Holiday's speciality. A machine like that was bound to have failsafes and backup routines. Even if he could find a way of tampering with it, it'd only restart itself and ...

And ...

Rex looked at the switches on the front of the machine. With his outstretched arm, he reached over and pressed the one marked "OFF". The machine's display went dark and Rex sat up. He yanked the wires from his chest.

'They just don't make torture devices like they

used to,' he muttered. He looked over at the metal door. 'And now,' he said, steadying himself, 'for the hard part.'

CHAPTER 12

REX TRIED THE DOOR. It was locked, but then, that wasn't exactly a surprise. If someone had gone to all the trouble of kidnapping him and attaching him to an electric shock machine, it was a pretty safe bet they'd remember to bolt the door, too.

He tried to summon his Smackhands, but his nanites still weren't responding. The effort of concentrating made his head spin. He had to lean against the wall to stop himself falling over.

He was in bad shape. His legs felt heavier than a broken Punk Buster and he was still shaking from the high voltage shocks he'd received. A locked metal door was the last thing he needed.

There was a keypad beside the door. Rex punched in a few numbers and hit a button marked "UNLOCK".

'Code not recognised,' chimed a robotic voice. 'Please try again.'

'Don't mind if I do,' said Rex. He tried several more combinations of numbers, but each one was met with the same response.

'Code not recognised. Please try again.'

'Ah, what's the use?' Rex sighed. 'This isn't getting me anywhere. There's only one thing for it.'

Rex stepped back, picked a spot beside the handle of the door, and kicked hard. A shudder of pain travelled along his leg and up the entire length of his spine. The door did not so much as budge.

'O-OK-K,' Rex stammered, his whole body vibrating. 'N-not my b-best idea.'

Hobbling, he turned around and cast his gaze across the rest of the room. He was secretly hoping there was another exit, one he just hadn't spotted yet. There wasn't. Aside from the door behind him, there was no other way in or out of the room.

His eyes fell on the machine that had electrocuted him. He had an urge to smash it, but there was something else, too. Something flickering at the very back of his tired and groggy brain. An idea.

The machine was attached to a metal stand, with four shopping trolley style wheels attached to the bottom. In his weakened state, it took all Rex's strength to roll the thing over to the door.

Pausing only to get his breath back, Rex attached the cables to the front of the keypad. As he connected the wires up, his hand brushed against a few of the door control's buttons.

'Code not recognised,' it said. 'Please try again.'

Rex grinned. 'Recognise *this*,' he said, and he flicked the switch to turn the shock machine back on.

A flash of blue light filled the room. There was a *sizzle*, then a *bang*, then a puff of grey smoke.

'Code recognised,' droned the voice. It sounded much slower than it had a moment ago. 'Have a nice daaaaaaaay.'

The voice slowed to a complete stop. With a *swish*, the metal door slid open, revealing a darkened corridor. Rex leaned out and glanced in both directions. Nothing moved in the shadows, but Rex had a feeling danger wasn't very far away.

He tried his builds again. Smackhands, Punk Busters, Boogie Pack — nothing. Unarmed and alone, he sidled out of the room, and began to make his way through the darkness.

Gradually, Rex's eyes began to adjust. The corridor had no windows, and the same peeling paint as the room he'd woken up in. Pipes ran along the walls, and he got the feeling he was in a basement, or some large underground complex.

The corridor turned sharply and Rex followed it, keeping low and close to the wall in case anyone was waiting up ahead. Squinting through the gloom he saw no one, but he did see some*thing*.

Another door blocked the way just a few metres ahead. He crept closer and examined it. This door was made of plain wood, with a metal handle about halfway up. There was no keypad beside it. There wasn't even a keyhole in the door itself and so, Rex guessed, it wasn't locked.

He pressed his ear against the wood; listened, but heard nothing. He was about to reach for the handle when the squeal of an alarm tore along the corridor. Red lights lit up the darkness, flashing on and off in time with the alarm. From behind him, back the way he'd come, he heard raised voices. Someone had realised he'd escaped!

There was no time for stealth now. Grabbing the handle, Rex turned it and yanked open the door.

A hulking creature loomed on the other side.

It flexed its long, deadly claws.

'Going somewhere?' it growled, and Rex finally realised why he had recognised that voice.

'Biowulf!' he hissed. Rex knew he was in no condition to fight Van Kleiss' second-in-command. Spinning on the spot, he prepared to run, but a four-armed girl blocked his escape. The girl peered at him through her matted curtain of black hair.

'And Breach, too,' Rex said. He smiled weakly. 'I'm guessing you guys didn't just drop by for a chat?'

Rex ducked as one of Breach's powerful fists smashed against the wall beside his head. Plaster dust rained down on the floor.

'No, didn't think so,' said Rex. He pointed over Breach's shoulder. 'Hey, look, it's the Easter Bunny.'

Breach turned and Rex took his chance. Shoving her aside he raced past her. 'Sucker!' he grinned. 'Easter was months ago!'

Sliding around the corner, Rex sped along the corridor. Behind him, he heard the clatter of Biowulf's metallic feet. 'After him!'

Rex groaned. Earlier, he'd thought there was no way his day could possibly get any worse, but he was

beginning to realise ....
    He was wrong!

CHAPTER 13

REX POWERED ALONG THE corridor, searching frantically for another way out. A shimmering red circle seemed to tear through the darkness up ahead. Rex recognised it at once as one of Breach's portals.

Throwing himself forwards, Rex slid, head-first, beneath the portal, just as Breach's arms reached out. He felt all twenty of her fingers grab at him, but she was too slow. Rolling, Rex sprang back to his feet and continued to race along the passageway.

Another corner loomed up ahead. Rex took it at full speed, battering against the wall as he hurled himself around. He stopped when he saw the corridor was filled with men in dirty lab coats. They glared at him over the tops of their thick glasses.

'Trust me, guys,' Rex growled, 'you do *not* want to get in my way right now.'

With an angry roar, Rex charged. The technicians all yelped with fright and did their best to get out of his way. Some pressed themselves against the walls, while others dropped to the floor, their hands over their head. Still others climbed onto the backs of their colleagues, doing everything they could to scramble out of Rex's path.

Rex hurtled through the gap. His legs felt wobbly and weak, and even running was taking everything he had. Fighting Biowulf and Breach wasn't an option.

With a final bound, Rex leapt over the last of the cowering technicians. As he sailed through the air, the darkness ahead of him became filled with a bright red glow.

'Aw, nuts,' Rex sighed, as a portal opened up directly in his path.

Instead of landing on the basement floor, Rex hit dirt. He rolled clumsily through a mound of soil, becoming tangled in the weeds and vines that grew from it.

Rex tried to scramble to his feet, but the last of his strength was fading fast. His legs shook and his arms trembled and he could do nothing to stop himself falling face down into the dirt.

A clawed hand caught him roughly by the back

of his jacket and hoisted him into the air. Rex saw Breach step through the portal. She was pushing a man in a lab coat ahead of her. The man wore a dark, sinister-looking mask that covered his entire head. Rex couldn't help but wonder what sort of face lurked under there.

'Let go of me,' Rex snapped. He flailed around, trying to break the grip on his back. Biowulf gave him a violent shake and Rex felt the world spin again.

'Cool it, runt,' Biowulf snarled. 'You've got an appointment with the boss.'

Rex was hoisted up onto Biowulf's shoulder. The hulking Evo carried him through the dark and twisting forest of Abysus, home of Rex's arch-enemy, Van Kleiss. He leapt easily over fallen logs and exposed roots, and Rex actually found himself feeling relieved that he wasn't being made to walk. In his current condition, he didn't think he'd have been able to make it all the way to ...

Van Kleiss' castle. It stood at the edge of the forest, but it looked as if it were being claimed by the trees. Roots and branches grew over the crumbling stone. Moss and ivy spread like a rash across the parapets.

Through the narrow windows, Rex could see nothing but darkness.

With a grunt of effort, Biowulf hoisted Rex higher on his shoulder and made his way towards the castle entrance.

'Hey, isn't there a movie on this flight?' Rex asked. 'Or some complimentary nibbles or something?'

'Shut up,' Biowulf growled.

'What's the matter? Am I getting too heavy for ya?' Rex grinned. He was doing his best to hide his fear. 'You know, I can't help thinking it would've been a lot easier if Breach had just made another portal.'

Biowulf stopped walking. Slowly, he turned and glared at Breach, who was still shoving the technician along ahead of her. Breach gave a slightly embarrassed shrug of her oversized upper arms, and a red hole appeared in the space directly ahead of the group.

'Wow,' said Rex, shaking his head. 'It's easy to see why Van Kleiss is the brains of the operation.'

With a growl, Biowulf dropped Rex to the ground. He opened his clawed hands wide and loomed over the fallen boy. 'Right, that's it,' he snarled. 'You're going *down*.'

Summoning all his strength, Rex dragged himself back to his feet. He met Biowulf's stare and shot it straight back at him. 'Bring it on, dog breath!'

'Uh ... pardon me?'

Biowulf and Rex turned to see who had spoken. The technician stood beside them, nervously wringing his hands.

'*What?*' they both asked at once.

'Well, it's just ... I mean, it may not be my place to ... to ...' He swallowed hard. 'I believe Mr Van Kleiss needs the boy unharmed.'

Biowulf's already narrow eyes narrowed even further. The technician seemed to shrink beneath his gaze.

'Um ... just saying,' the man in the mask whimpered.

'What do you mean, *he needs me unharmed*?' Rex demanded. 'Why does he need me?'

'None of your business!' Biowulf barked.

Rex frowned. 'It's totally my business. Think about it.'

This seemed to confuse the wolf-like Evo. He shook his head, then gave Rex a shove towards Breach's portal. 'Then see for yourself!'

In a flash of red light, Rex found himself standing inside a room in the castle. The same roots and branches grew up the walls here, but it was what was in the middle of the room that was holding Rex's attention.

Van Kleiss was lying on a hospital-style bed, connected to four machines, not unlike the ones Rex had been hooked up to.

As Rex stepped through the portal, his arch-enemy raised his head and smiled. 'Ah, Rex,' Van Kleiss said. 'I hoped you'd come.'

'You didn't exactly leave me much choice!'

'Yes, please accept my apologies for that,' Van Kleiss said. 'But it was very important I got you here. In fact, you might say it was a matter of life and death.'

CHAPTER 14

A FIRM SHOVE FROM Biowulf sent Rex stumbling towards Van Kleiss.

'That's enough, Biowulf,' Van Kleiss warned. 'Rex is our guest here, not our prisoner.'

'I know how you treat your guests,' Rex said. 'I think I'd rather be a prisoner.'

Van Kleiss opened his mouth, but before he could speak he was gripped by a violent fit of coughing. When the coughing eventually subsided, Van Kleiss lay back on the bed and let out a low groan.

'What's the matter?' Rex asked. 'Has poor little Van Kleissy caught a cold?'

The villain smiled, grimly. 'Something like that.'

'OK, so you got me here. Now, tell me what you want so I can say "no" and then go home.'

'I need your help, Rex,' Van Kleiss said.

'No,' said Rex. 'See ya.' He turned to leave, only to find Biowulf blocking his path.

'Please, at least hear me out,' Van Kleiss said.

'If you still wish to leave after that, so be it.'

Rex turned back to the bed. He'd never seen Van Kleiss looking so weak. Now would've been the perfect time to take him down for good, if it weren't for the fact that Rex was still drained, too.

'You got one minute,' Rex told him. 'Then I'm outta here.'

'Very well,' Van Kleiss said. 'That is a most generous offer.'

'Fifty-five seconds,' Rex said. 'Start talking.'

'I am dying, Rex.'

Rex shrugged. 'And that's my problem because ...?'

'I know we've had our differences, Rex,' Van Kleiss wheezed. 'But this is my darkest hour. My nanites have become unstable. My strength has left me. We may be enemies, but surely you could not stand back and allow me to die?'

Rex pretended to think about this. 'You know, I think I could?' he said at last. 'Yeah. I have no problem with that. Now, are we finished, or was there something else?'

'No,' said Van Kleiss, closing his eyes slowly. 'That was all.'

'OK, well see you around,' Rex said, sidestepping Biowulf and heading for the door. 'Or I guess I won't.'

'How's the amnesia, Rex?'

Right by the doorway, Rex stopped. He didn't turn around.

'Memories still hazy?' Van Kleiss asked. 'Still struggling to piece together your past?'

Rex turned back to face the bed. Van Kleiss had a satisfied smirk on his face. Beside him, the technician and breach were wheeling another bed into position.

'That's a shame,' Van Kleiss continued. 'If only there was someone who knew everything about your history. Someone who knew about your family, even.' He raised his golden clawed hand and stroked his chin, thoughtfully. 'Oh, wait,' he said, 'there is. *Me.*'

Another bout of coughing echoed around the dank stone room. The technician was busily attaching complicated-looking machines to the second bed, but Rex was too fixed on Van Kleiss to notice.

'It's a shame I'm dying, really,' the villain said. 'Because it means all that knowledge about your family will die with me. And do you know what that means, Rex?'

'What?' Rex spat.

'You'll *never* find out what happened to them.'

Rex threw himself at Van Kleiss, fists raised. Biowulf moved to block him, but Van Kleiss waved his henchman away. 'Do your worst, Rex,' he said, calmly. 'It cannot be any worse than the fate that already awaits me.'

Rex punched the bed beside Van Kleiss' head. He wanted to hurt him – badly – but everything the villain had said was true. If he died, then Rex would never find out about his past.

Still, he knew Van Kleiss and The Pack weren't to be trusted. His body was still weak and his brain was still fuzzy, but he had a nagging feeling that what he was about to do was crazy.

'OK,' Rex said, through gritted teeth. 'What do you need me to do?'

Van Kleiss had to fight to hold back his smile. 'A few nanites, that's all I need,' he said. 'Just a few. They should help stabilise my own and allow me to bring them back under control.'

Rex looked at the bed beside Van Kleiss. 'And after that, you're going to tell me about my family.'

'But of course,' Van Kleiss nodded. 'A fair trade. You have my word that I will tell you everything.'

'If you don't, you have *my* word that I'll hurt you so bad you'll wish I'd let you die.'

Van Kleiss couldn't contain his smile any longer. 'Oh Rex,' he said. 'I so love our little chats.'

With a final glance at Biowulf and Breach, Rex slid up onto the bed. The man in the mask hurriedly stuck half a dozen wires to him. They matched the wires that were already attached to Van Kleiss.

'Everything ready?' Biowulf asked.

The technician flipped a few switches. Every one of the machines began to emit a low humming sound. 'Ready,' he nodded.

'I promise you, you will not regret this, Rex,' Van Kleiss said. 'I owe you a great debt.'

'Yeah, yeah,' Rex said. 'Just make sure you pay up afterwards.'

'Oh, I will, I will,' Van Kleiss said. His face darkened and something wicked glinted behind his eyes. 'Now, you might want to brace yourself, because this is *really* going to hurt!'

And with that, the machine screamed into life.

CHAPTER 15

EX'S BACK ARCHED AS a shock of agony tore through his central nervous system. His teeth clamped together and his limbs went rigid. It was almost the same feeling as when he'd been hit by the electric shock machine, only much, *much* worse.

'Wh-what are you d-doing?' he managed to hiss. It took all his effort to turn his head towards Van Kleiss. The villain's muscles stood in knots and his face was a bright red. It was clear that he was in as much pain as Rex was, but it didn't seem to bother him. If anything, the maniac looked like he was *enjoying* it.

'Y-Yes!' he cried. 'More power. *More power!*'

The technician cranked up the dial on one of the machines attached to Rex. Another wave of pain washed over him, forcing a cry from his lips. Over it, he heard Van Kleiss' low, sickening laugh.

'Can you feel it, Rex? Can you feel the nanites being torn from within you?'

'Y-you tricked m-me!'

'You didn't exactly make it hard!' Van Kleiss laughed. 'Full power!' he demanded.

'B-but sir,' the technician stammered, 'any more and the results could be –'

Van Kleiss' face twisted in rage. 'I said *full power!*'

The technician didn't dare protest again. Instead, he turned the control dial all the way up to one hundred. The machine let out a high whine and a blinding white flash filled Rex's vision.

The pain stopped, and for a moment, Rex thought he might be dead. But then his vision began to clear, and he saw Biowulf and Breach standing over him, peering down.

'What did you do?' he croaked. He'd been weak before he climbed onto the bed, but now it was taking all his effort just to stay awake. 'W-What did you do to me?'

'Did it work?' Biowulf asked. He looked from Rex to Van Kleiss and back again. Finally, he turned to the technician.

'I ... uh ... I believe it *may* have been at least a partial, uh, partial ...'

'Oh, it worked,' said Van Kleiss. His voice no longer

sounded frail and his body looked stronger than ever. 'I can feel it. I can feel *them*. All those nanites. Every single one of them.'

Rex tried to move, but his body was too weak. He felt strange in a way he couldn't really describe. An itch burned at his left hand, from his wrist all the way to the tips of his fingers.

'But don't take *my* word for it,' Van Kleiss said. 'Allow me to demonstrate.'

The villain looked down at his feet. His brow furrowed for a moment, as if he were concentrating. Then, with a *clank*, a pair of mechanical legs appeared below Van Kleiss' knees. Rex recognised his Punk Busters right away.

'No!' he gasped.

'Oh, *yes*,' Van Kleiss cackled. He retracted the Punk Busters and out came the Smackhands. He banged the metal fists together and the sound echoed around the castle. 'I'm going to enjoy playing with these,' Van Kleiss said. He jumped down from the bed.

'Looking good,' said Biowulf, nodding his approval.

'Thank you, Biowulf. And thank *you*,' he said,

turning to the technician. 'You have done well. The process was a complete success.'

'Yes, uh, well ... *mostly* a success,' the masked man mumbled.

Van Kleiss hesitated. '*Mostly?*'

'There's a chance that something went, uh, went wrong, sir. The machine was never really designed to go all the way up to a hundred. There may be ... side effects.'

'What sort of side effects?' asked Van Kleiss, his voice as cold as ice.

Rex let out a yelp of shock as Van Kleiss' golden claw appeared where his left hand had been.

'Those sort of side effects,' the technician whimpered. 'You were pulling in his nanites so fast there was no room for yours to adjust. They, uh, they had to go *somewhere.*'

'And they went into him,' Biowulf realised.

'I haven't stolen his nanites, I've swapped mine for his,' Van Kleiss said. 'No matter.' He flexed both his machine arms. 'I'd say I got the better side of the deal. Wouldn't you, Rex?'

Rex was still staring at the claw where his hand

should have been, barely able to believe what he was seeing. He looked up as Van Kleiss loomed over him.

'These abilities of yours, Rex, they're really quite remarkable. I mean, don't get me wrong, these ... *toys* of yours are all well and good, but that's not why I took your nanites. Do you want to know why I took them, Rex?'

'You're going to tell me anyway,' Rex replied.

'I took your nanites because they will let me absorb other nanites.' His face twisted into a wicked grin. 'I'm going to do you a favour, Rex. I'm going to do your job for you. I'm going to travel the world, curing Evos. And with each Evo I cure, the more powerful I will become! Nothing will be able to stop me. *Nothing*. What do you have to say about that?'

'Sorry,' Rex shrugged. 'Wasn't listening. I was doing something else.'

'Doing what?'

Rex grinned. '*This*.'

A thick vine snaked up from the floor at Van Kleiss' feet and wrapped around his legs. With a sharp *yank* it pulled him through the floor.

Rex stumbled down from the bed and turned to

face Biowulf and Breach. He raised Van Kleiss' claw and pointed it at the villains. 'Now,' he said, swallowing back the pain. 'Let's see what else this thing can do.'

CHAPTER 16

DR HOLIDAY PULLED OUT her desk drawers and shook the contents into a plastic bag. Most of the equipment was owned by Providence, but the drawers were where she kept her own personal belongings. When they were empty, she stacked the drawers on top of the desk, picked up the bag, and made for the door.

White Knight's face filled the view screen before her. His eyes went briefly to the bag. 'You're not seriously going through with this?' he asked. 'What about all your work?'

'I'll keep working,' Holiday said. 'Just not here. And not for you.'

'What you do here is important,' White Knight reminded her.

'And what about Rex? Isn't he important? After everything he's done, you really expect me just to abandon him?'

The door to the lab slid open and Agent Six

strode in. Dr Holiday gripped her bag tighter. 'Don't even think about trying to stop me, Six,' she warned.

'Wouldn't dream of it,' Six told her. 'I just came to tell White Knight something.'

'Oh?' said White Knight. 'And what's that?'

Six turned to the screen. 'I quit.'

'What? But you can't quit!' White Knight gasped.

'I can't leave Rex out there alone, either,' Six replied. Even without looking, he could picture the smile on Holiday's face. 'So it doesn't look like I have a lot of choice.'

White Knight stared at them both in turn. 'What? But ...' He gave a loud sigh of irritation. 'Very well. Gather a team. Take the Keep. Go to Silicon Valley. See what you can find.'

'And tanks,' Six suggested. 'We'll need tanks.'

'Very well,' White Knight said. 'Just be quick.'

The screen went dark. 'Thank you, Six,' said Dr Holiday.

'Don't mention it. Now let's move.' He made for the door. Dr Holiday dropped her back and hurried after him.

'Do you really think we'll need *tanks*?' she asked.

'You can never have too many tanks,' Six replied, before the door swished closed behind them.

With a whine of engines, the Keep touched down in a wide plaza right in the heart of Silicon Valley. The landing ramp folded out from within the aircraft. Agent Six and a platoon of Agents marched down it.

'Spread out,' Six ordered. 'Look for signs of Rex.'

'What sort of signs, sir?' an Agent asked.

Six thought back to all of Rex's previous missions. 'Needless destruction. Reckless endangerment. Sarcastic backchat. The usual.'

As the Agents scattered, Dr Holiday joined Six on the ramp. She had a scanning device in her hand and was studying its screen closely.

'Anything?' asked Six.

Dr Holiday shook her head. 'Nothing yet. No Evo activity detected at all.' She looked up at Six, her face suddenly pale. 'What if we're too late? What if we don't find him?'

'Don't worry,' Six told her. His eyes were fixed on a swirling circle of red that had just opened up further along the plaza. 'I think we just did.'

A flailing figure fell through the portal and landed awkwardly on the ground. Rex's face was bruised and bleeding, and his clothes were torn. He raised his head and looked up at the Keep through swollen eyes.

'Rex!' Dr Holiday yelped. She hurried down the ramp and across the plaza. She was almost at Rex's side when a Smackhand appeared through the portal. It slammed down onto Rex's back, driving him hard against the concrete.

The portal widened and Van Kleiss stepped through. Dr Holiday's eyes were drawn to the mechanical arms the villain wielded. Only then did she spot the golden claw where Rex's own left hand should have been.

'What did you do to him?' Holiday demanded.

'Nothing, Doctor,' Van Kleiss replied. He caught Rex by one leg and hoisted him higher into the air. 'At least, nothing compared to what I'm *about* to do.'

'What you're about to do is put the kid down and surrender quietly,' Agent Six said, stepping in front of Dr Holiday.

'Oh? And why would I do that?'

'Because I'm asking you nicely,' said Six.

Van Kleiss laughed. 'In that case, I don't think I'll bother.'

With a *snink*, Agent Six's swords slid down his sleeves and into his hands. 'You know,' he began, 'I was hoping you'd say that.'

'Nice swords,' Van Kleiss said. He released his grip on Rex as the Smackhands pulled back into his body. The Big Freakin' Sword clanked out in their place. 'But mine's bigger than yours.'

Agent Six shook his head. 'I don't think so.'

There was a loud rumbling sound and five Providence tanks rolled out from within the Keep. Van Kleiss looked around. The Providence Agents stood in a circle around him. Every one of them had their weapon trained on him, their fingers poised on their triggers.

'Now, we can do this the easy way, or we can do it the hard way,' Six said. 'Either one suits me fine.' He turned just slightly and whispered to Holiday. 'When this kicks off, get Rex into the Keep and get out of here.'

'Understood.'

Six turned his attention back to Van Kleiss. 'So, what's it to be?'

Van Kleiss flicked his wrist. The blade of the Big Freakin' Sword began to spin like a buzz-saw. 'I think,' he grinned, 'we'll try the hard way.'

PROVIDENCE TANK EXPLODED as a blast from the Slam Cannon hit it head on. Van Kleiss took aim at another of the vehicles.

'You know, I don't think I've had this much fun in a long time,' he said, before another cannon blast reduced the second tank to a ball of flame.

'Take him down!' Agent Six bellowed. The sound of machine-gun fire ripped through the air as every one of the Agents opened fire.

Van Kleiss spun, the Slam Cannon already transforming into the Boogie Pack. The bullets whistled harmlessly beneath him as he launched himself into the air.

On the ground below, Providence Agents began to fall, struck by the bullets intended for Van Kleiss. 'Too easy,' the villain crowed.

A fast-moving shape in a dark green suit landed on his back. 'Don't speak too soon,' said Agent Six. He jammed a sword into the Boogie Pack's turbine engines. The spinning turbine blades stopped instantly. Van Kleiss cried out in shock as they began to plunge towards the ground.

A split-second before they hit, Van Kleiss' legs morphed into the Punk Busters. The ground cracked into a wide spiderweb pattern as the mechanical feet slammed down.

The sudden landing jarred Agent Six and sent him sprawling. He threw himself over Rex, shielding him from what was about to happen next.

'Now!' he barked into his communicator. There was a sound like thunder as one of the remaining tanks opened fire. A rocket streaked across the plaza towards Van Kleiss.

A Punk Buster lifted at the last possible moment, delivering a powerful kick to the underside of the missile. It flipped upwards, end over end, before exploding in a fiery blast.

Van Kleiss stepped from the smoke and fixed his gaze on the tank that had attacked him. 'Now you've gone and made me mad,' he growled. Blinded by anger, he charged at the tank, leaving Agent Six free to drag Rex to safety.

Dr Holiday hurried over to help Six carry Rex to the Keep. As they walked, Agent Six contacted White Knight and Providence HQ. 'Requesting back-up,' he said. 'Van Kleiss is on the rampage and we have a lot of Agents down.'

'Can't *you* deal with it, Agent Six?' White Knight asked.

'Negative, sir,' Six replied. He looked down at Rex, who was now only barely conscious. 'I've got more important things to worry about.'

'I got a bad feeling about this,' said Bobo. He was standing beside Rex's bed, cautiously prodding at the golden claw on the boy's hand. 'It ain't right, I tells ya.'

'I'll second that,' Agent Six nodded. He watched Dr Holiday as she ran more tests. From the look on her face, he could tell she wasn't making much progress. 'Problems?' he asked.

'One or two,' Holiday admitted. 'I don't understand, it's like Rex and Van Kleiss swapped nanites, but I don't even know if that's possible.'

'I give you Exhibit A,' said Bobo, pointing to the

claw. 'Let's go with "it's possible". What we gonna do about it?'

'Honestly? I have no idea,' said Holiday. 'Van Kleiss' nanites appear to be dangerously weakened, and without the soil he – I mean, *Rex* – is powerless.'

'So, what are you saying?' asked Six.

'I'm saying that if we try to help him, there's a good chance Rex won't survive.'

'What kinda villain has power over soil, anyhow?' grunted Bobo. 'I mean, talk about lame.'

An urgent crackle from the lab's communicator interrupted them. 'Van Kleiss has overpowered remaining Agents,' hissed a voice through the static. In the background, there was the unmistakeable sound of screaming. 'He's found an Evo and absorbed its nanites. Something's happening to him. Something –'

There was a sudden cry from the speaker, and then the communicator fell silent again.

Bobo winced. 'You don't think he heard me call him lame, do ya?'

Dr Holiday looked worried. 'If Van Kleiss continues absorbing nanites he could theoretically keep getting stronger,' she said. 'Then there'll be no way to stop him.'

'And to think, we used to worry about him when he just had the nature powers,' Bobo said. 'Hey, wait a minute.'

'What is it?' asked Six.

'Somethin's happening in my brain,' Bobo told them. 'Might be a migraine, or it might be ...' He clicked his fingers. 'An idea. Bobo's got an idea.'

'You do?' asked Dr Holiday. 'What is it?'

'You're not seriously going to listen to the monkey?' Six asked.

'At this point, I'm open to anything,' Holiday said. 'What's your idea, Bobo?'

'The Petting Zoo,' Bobo announced. He grinned at them, proudly.

'I knew it,' Six said. 'Never take advice from a primate.'

'I ain't finished,' Bobo told him. 'The Petting Zoo, it's full of Evo animals, right? Which means it's full of *nature*. Well, nature that's been messed up by nanites, anyhow.'

'What's your point?' Six asked.

'Van Kleiss' nanites respond to nature. Our boy

there is currently stuffed to the gunnels with Van Kleiss' nanites.'

'You think maybe the nanites will draw strength from those in the Petting Zoo?' said Dr Holiday.

'Gotta be worth a try, right?' Bobo shrugged.

Agent Six turned to Holiday. 'Could it work?'

'Maybe,' Holiday replied. 'I think ... maybe it could.'

In a single fluid movement, Six hoisted Rex up onto his shoulder. 'Then what are we waiting for?' he said. 'Let's move!'

'**S**TAY STILL, I'M HERE to help you,' Van Kleiss urged. 'You'll thank me for this later.'

A little round Evo, about the size of a large beach ball, screamed in fear as Van Kleiss hoisted it up into the air. The Boogie Pack's turbines whined loudly, struggling with the weight. Van Kleiss had absorbed hundreds of thousands of nanites in the past few hours. His body was bulging and swollen with them.

But he wasn't finished yet.

Gritting his teeth, Van Kleiss began to draw the Evo's nanites out from within it. His already bloated limbs became fatter still. His stomach expanded, popping a button on his coat. Held in his fat hands, the Evo gradually became human again.

Van Kleiss looked down at the terrified young woman he now carried. 'Thank you, my dear,' he said, licking his lips. And then he opened his arms and let the woman fall.

The air whistled around her, drowning out her

screams as she plunged towards the distant ground. She closed her eyes, bracing herself for the end.

WHUMPF!

The woman crashed down onto a cushion of air. It deflated slowly, lowering her gently back down to Earth. The gloved hand of a Providence Agent reached down and helped her up.

'Th-thank you,' she whimpered.

The Agent nodded. 'All part of the service, ma'am.'

Far overhead, Van Kleiss wobbled unsteadily across the sky, away from the city and on towards the world beyond.

THWIP!

A look of surprise flashed across the face of an Evo rabbit as a tranquiliser dart buried itself in the animal's neck. It stood perfectly still for a moment, before toppling sideways onto the ground. Thirty metres away, Dr Holiday lowered the rifle.

'Nice shooting, Doc,' said Bobo, nodding his approval.

'You sure I can't interest you in working as a field

agent?' Six asked. 'We could use someone who can actually hit what they're aiming at once in a while.'

'No thanks,' said Holiday. 'I wouldn't suit the uniform.'

'Come on, Doc,' said Bobo, looking her up and down. 'We all know that ain't true.'

Dr Holiday didn't reply. Instead, she lead Bobo and Agent Six across to the fallen rabbit. Rex hung limply over Six's shoulder. His faint groans were the only sign that he was still alive.

Bobo stood guard with his laser pistols while Holiday and Six propped Rex up next to the sleeping bunny. It was as large as a Great Dane dog, with metre-long ears and teeth like razors.

'Rex, can you hear me?' asked Holiday, leaning down so her face was next to him. A low moan escaped Rex's lips, but otherwise he showed no sign of having heard. 'Rex, you need to wake up!'

Six took hold of Rex's hands and placed them on the rabbit. 'Up and at 'em, soldier,' he barked. 'Or you're going to have *me* to answer to.'

One of Rex's eyes twitched. A breath hissed out from within him.

'Maybe this ain't gonna work, after all,' Bobo admitted.

'Wait!' whispered Holiday. 'Something's happening. Look!'

On the mud-slicked floor of the Petting Zoo, the bunny had started to shrink. Its coarse, wiry fur was becoming softer and fluffier. Its ears were getting smaller by the second, and its teeth looked nowhere near as deadly as they did just a moment ago.

It was working – Rex was absorbing the animal's nanites!

'That's my boy!' Bobo smirked, seeing the colour slowly return to Rex's cheeks. 'I knew it'd work. Am I a genius or what?'

With a sudden gasp, Rex woke up. His eyed darted left and right and his nose twitched, like a rabbit sniffing for danger. Finally, he focused on Holiday. 'Ah ... what's up, Doc?' he asked, hoarsely.

Holiday hugged him. 'Welcome back, Rex,' she said. Rex lay there, enjoying the hug, but Agent Six quickly ruined the mood.

'You look like death, kid,' he said. 'We'd better get you some more nanites.'

'Where from?' Rex asked.

Six gestured around at the Petting Zoo, and at the many shapes lurking in the trees and bushes. 'Take your pick.'

The Boogie Pack's twin engines finally gave up, and Van Kleiss bounced hard against the desert floor. He had just absorbed the nanites of a three-headed bat-like Evo, and his body now resembled a balloon filled with runny custard. It made a nasty squelching sound as he rolled down a sand dune.

'N-need m-more nanites,' he hissed as he tried to raise himself up on his bulging legs. He concentrated, trying to summon the Punk Busters, but the mechanical legs wouldn't appear. The vast amount of new nanites he'd absorbed were interfering with his control over those he'd stolen from Rex.

Through sheer force of will, he was finally able to stand. But standing was all he could do. His legs were too heavy to lift. His feet became uncomfortably hot and he realised his immense weight was making him sink down into the sand. All of a sudden, he found himself regretting those last hundred thousand nanites.

A vast shadow passed across him. Van Kleiss craned his blubbery neck to find the Keep hovering in the sky directly above him.

On board, a Providence lieutenant barked orders. 'Lower a hook. Winch him up.' He peered down at the blob, slowly sinking into the desert floor below. 'On second thoughts,' he said, 'make that *two* hooks.'

'**H**OW YOU FEELING, KID?' asked Bobo. It was obvious, though, that Rex was feeling *much* better than he had for a long time.

He was standing up for one thing, and smiling for another. He had cured eight different Evo animals now, and with each nanite he'd absorbed, the weakness that had been crippling him had faded.

'I'm feeling great,' Rex said. He flexed Van Kleiss' golden claw. 'Although this still feels kinda weird.'

'That's only to be expected,' Agent Six said.

'And I have an overwhelming urge to lick my own butt,' Rex added.

Six blinked. 'OK. That one I didn't expect.'

'Ah, it's just the animal nanites,' Bobo shrugged. 'Happens to me all the time. I say go for it, kid.'

Agent Six shuddered. 'I say *don't*. Ever. In fact, that's an order.'

Rex fired off a mock-salute, and almost knocked himself out in the process. He glared at his metallic hand. 'Man, I have *got* to get rid of this thing.'

'Dr Holiday's gone back to the lab to work on it,' Six said. He paused, listening to a voice in his ear. 'In fact, I believe she's making progress right now.'

The door to Holiday's lab slid open. Rex scampered in and leapt up onto the desk. Six and Bobo entered the room just behind him.

'Down off the furniture, Rex,' Six told him.

With a jump, Rex landed on the floor beside him.

'Good boy,' Six said. He tossed a biscuit into the air. Rex caught it in his mouth.

Dr Holiday watched them with growing amusement. 'The animal nanites?' she asked.

'Trust me,' said Six. 'You do *not* want to know.'

Holiday nodded. 'Well, thanks for coming so quickly. There's something I want to show you. Or rather, some*one*.'

She pulled away a folding screen, revealing the bulging frame of Van Kleiss. He was lying on two beds, pushed close together. His blubbery skin hung down over the sides in huge folds.

'Whoa!' cried Rex. 'Who ate all the nanites?'

'Laugh all you like, Rex,' Van Kleiss hissed. 'I still have your nanites, and you're still stuck with mine. Away from Abysus, the powers you have now are useless.' A grin spread across his puffed-up face. 'Face it, Rex, I've won!'

'The only thing you look like you could win is a pie-eating contest,' Rex said. He gave the villain's leg a prod. It wobbled like jelly. 'Ugh. Seriously, Van Kleiss, you've *really* let yourself go.'

Van Kleiss turned to Dr Holiday. 'You will take me to Purgatory and offload the nanites,' he told her. 'You will restore me to my normal size.'

'Oh?' said Dr Holiday. 'And why would I go and do a thing like that?'

Van Kleiss' eyes went wide with horror. 'You can't just leave me like this! It is Providence's duty to help Evos wherever it can. You *will* help me!'

'No,' said Holiday.

'*No?*'

'That's what the lady said,' Rex grinned.

'But ... but you *can't!*'

Dr Holiday smiled. 'Tell you what. Give Rex his

nanites back, and I'll think about helping you.'

Van Kleiss' eyes narrowed. 'Never! You will help me because it is your duty to help me. What would White Knight say if he knew you were blackmailing a poor, helpless Evo like this?'

'Let's ask him,' said Six, as a familiar face appeared on the lab's video screen.

'Someone called?' asked White Knight, gruffly.

'White Knight,' began Van Kleiss. 'Your subordinates are refusing to help me. Dr Holiday is shirking her responsibilities and going against everything Providence stands for.'

'Really?' asked White Knight. 'Dr Holiday,' he said, sharply.

'Yes, sir?'

White Knight gave her a curt nod. 'Keep up the good work.'

The screen went dark. All eyes in the room turned to Van Kleiss.

'Now then,' Holiday said. 'About that transfer?'

Van Kleiss glared at them all in turn. Hatred burned behind his eyes. At last, though, he gave a sigh. 'Fine,' he muttered. 'Someone pass me the phone.'

Rex lay on another bed just a few metres from Van Kleiss. Breach and Biowulf lurked at the back of the lab, guarded by Agent Six, Bobo and a dozen Providence agents.

Rex winced as Van Kleiss' masked technician connected them both up to the transfer machines. 'This is going to hurt again, isn't it?'

The technician shook his head. 'It shouldn't,' he said. 'I've adjusted the design slightly. You shouldn't feel a thing. '

MOOOOOOO!

The technician hesitated. 'Did ... did you just moo like a cow?'

Rex blushed. 'Animal nanites,' he said. 'Sorry.'

'Can we *please* get this over with?' Van Kleiss spat.

The technician nodded. 'It's just a straight reversal. It ... it shouldn't take more than a few seconds.'

With a flick of a switch, the technician activated the machines. Van Kleiss let out a howl of pain.

'I thought you said we wouldn't feel a thing?' said Rex, watching his arch-enemy squirm and twist.

The technician shrugged. 'I said *you* wouldn't feel a thing.'

Rex smiled, then watched in amazement as the golden claw retracted back into his arm. A moment later, it began to reappear, but this time it was back with its rightful owner.

Rex raised an arm. In the blink of an eye it became a mechanical fist. 'And the Smackhands are back in business,' he announced, happily. With a *click*, the technician switched the machine off.

'I have upheld my end of the bargain,' Van Kleiss growled. 'Now uphold yours.'

Agent Six approached the bed. 'We will. I'll arrange for you to be taken to Purgatory Base for nanite offloading.'

'Hey, Six,' said Rex, holding back a grin. 'Isn't Purgatory closed for a few days? Didn't I hear that somewhere?'

'Actually, now I think about it, you're right,' said Six, going along with the joke. 'You'll have to wait a week or so,' he told Van Kleiss. 'Two weeks at most'

'You tricked me!' Van Kleiss spat. 'I shall find a way to offload the nanites myself. *Breach!*'

A portal opened up on the floor beside Van Kleiss' bed. Another opened beside Biowulf and Breach. They stepped through it and disappeared.

'You, too,' growled Van Kleiss, pointing a clawed finger at the technician.

'N-no thanks,' the technician stammered. 'I think I'll stay here.'

Van Kleiss scowled. 'So be it,' he said, then he rolled sideways off the bed and fell through the portal.

CHAPTER 20

THE TECHNICIAN STOOD BEHIND his machine. Only his eyes were visible through his mask. They flitted nervously across the faces of the other people in the room.

'I'm ... I'm sorry for the trouble I caused,' he said. 'It wasn't me, it was ... it was the mask.'

Reaching around to the back of his head, the technician undid the mask. Rex braced himself, expecting to see the twisted face of an Evo creature looking back at him. Instead, he saw the face of a young man, not much older than himself. A scattering of soil fell out of the mask as he tipped it upside down.

'Van Kleiss, he put his soil inside the mask. He ... he used it to make me do things. He controlled me.'

'Mind control soil?' said Rex. 'You've gotta be kidding me!'

'The control was broken when his nanites swapped with yours,' the technician explained. 'If I'd have gone back, he'd have been able to take control of me again. So I decided to stay here, and face whatever punishment you deemed appropriate.'

Dr Holiday and Six exchanged a glance. Six nodded.

'How does forty-eight hours a week on minimum wage, with a *terrible* staff canteen sound as a punishment?' Holiday asked.

The technician's eyes went wide. 'You're offering me a job?'

'I'm offering you a job,' Dr Holiday nodded. 'You can help keep our equipment running. How does that sound?'

'Thank you! I can't believe –'

White Knight's face appeared on the screen once again. 'Six. Holiday. Rex,' he barked. 'I want a word with you. The rest of you, leave. Now.'

When Bobo and the others had left the room, White Knight cleared his throat. 'It appears that I owe you an apology, Dr Holiday,' he said.

Dr Holiday could hardly believe her ears. 'Uh, sorry, sir, but did you just say –?'

'No need to rub it in, Doctor,' White Knight

replied. 'You were right. I was wrong. Recovering Rex should have been our priority. Had I listened to you, none of this would have happened.'

'Let's all agree now that recovering Rex should *always* be our priority,' said Rex. 'Can we vote that in right now?'

Agent Six spoke to Holiday, but didn't turn to look at her. 'And, uh, sorry from me, too. I should've gone along with you from the start.'

'Look, I'm voting "yes",' chirped Rex, raising his hand. 'Anyone else?'

Dr Holiday smiled warmly. 'Apology accepted,' she said.

'You all did a great job out there today ,' White Knight told them. 'But Rex, you've been through a lot. I'm ordering you to rest up for a few weeks.'

Rex's ears picked up. 'Rest?' he said. 'You mean I'm getting time off?'

'That's exactly what I mean,' White Knight nodded. 'I've arranged for a selection of movies and video games to be sent up to your room. I believe Noah's out collecting pizzas now.'

Rex bounced up and down excitedly on the spot.

'You know, White Knight, no matter what Six says about you, I think you're awesome!'

Still bouncing up and down, Rex threw his arms around Six and Holiday. Turning his face to theirs, he licked both of their cheeks in turn. 'Thanks, guys!' he cried, before bounding off towards the door.

Six wiped the slobber off his cheek with his sleeve. 'Tell me the effects of those animal nanites are going to wear off soon,' he said.

'Uh, yeah,' Dr Holiday said, unable to resist the urge to laugh. 'They will. I *hope!*'

TOTAL RECALL

Test your memory of 'The Trade' with these eight tricky questions. Remember: no checking back!

1
Rex fights the slug-Evo in which city?
a. San Jose
b. Santa Barbara
c. San Francisco

2
What kind of Evo floors Rex in Fremont?
a. Slug
b. Scorpion
c. Spider

3
Who helps Dr Holiday discover the reason for Rex's malfunctions?
a. Agent Six
b. Bobo Haha
c. Noah

4
What is the highest voltage of electric shock Rex receives in the lab?
a. 900 volts
b. 800 volts
c. 700 volts

5 Who attempts to carry Rex to Castle Van Kleiss?
a. Skalamander
b. Biowulf
c. Breach

6 Which of Rex's machines does Van Kleiss demonstrate first after the trade of nanites?
a. Smackhands
b. Boogie Pack
c. Punk Busters

7 Where does Bobo suggest Rex is taken to recover from the trade?
a. Purgatory
b. Paradise
c. The Petting Zoo

8 What kind of Evo animal has its nanites absorbed by Rex first?
a. rabbit
b. dog
c. chimp

Answers: 1. c, 2. b, 3. c, 4. a,
5. b, 6. c, 7. c, 8. a.

Read an exclusive sneak preview of
GENERATOR REX: MIRROR MIRROR

'**C**OME ON, REX, it'll be awesome!'

Rex shrugged and jabbed his thumbs against the video game controller in his hands. On screen, a zombie's head exploded. '*This* is already awesome,' he said. 'It couldn't be any ... awesomer.'

'That's not even a word,' Noah said. 'And, seriously, sitting around playing video games all night? That's your idea of fun?'

'Yes,' Rex nodded. He stuffed some popcorn into his mouth. 'Yes, it is.'

Noah leaned forward in his chair and tried to make his friend see sense. 'I'm going to spell it out to you, Rex. It's a *fun ... fair.*'

'That's not spelling it out, that's just saying it slowly,' Rex mumbled, through a mouthful of popcorn kernels.

'That's not the point! The point is, it's got fun right there in the title. *Fun* fair. Does "video game" have the word "fun" in the title?' Noah asked.

'Not the last time I checked,' Rex replied. He shot a zombie through the knees and watched it fall, face-first, onto the ground.

'Nice shot,' Noah admitted, grudgingly.

'Thanks. I'm all about the knee-shots.'

An idea struck Noah. 'There'll be zombie-shooting at the fair,' he said.

Rex raised an eyebrow. 'Really?'

Noah sighed. 'No, not really. I made that up. But there'll be other stuff. *Better* than zombie-killing.'

'Nothing's better than zombie-killing,' Rex told him.

'Oh yeah? What about roller-coasters? And chair-o-planes? And bungee drops? They've got something called the Wheel of Terror.' Noah said it again for emphasis. '*The Wheel of Terror*, Rex! I don't even know what that is, but I don't think I can live another day without finding out.'

The action on screen froze as Rex hit the pause button on the control pad. 'You know I can turn whole parts of my body into machines, right?'

Noah nodded. 'Of course I know!'

'I've got the Boogie Pack that lets me fly, the Rex

Ride that lets me go faster than a racing car ...'

'Yeah, so?'

'Then there's the others, too. Punk Busters, Smackhands, a giant sword, a crazy-cool cannon that can shoot pretty much anything ...'

'I know all this!' Noah said. 'What's your point?'

'My point is, how is a roller-coaster supposed to compete with all that? Why would I bother going up and down and around on a metal track when I can do all that in mid-air, like, a thousand times faster, and without having to pay for it?'

Noah looked annoyed. 'Uh, well, maybe because some of us *can't* do any of that stuff? You might get to zip around the place going all high-tech all the time, but what about me?'

Rex saw the hurt on his friend's face. 'Hey, Noah, I'm sorry,' he said. 'I guess I didn't think of it like that.'

'Yeah, well, don't worry about it,' Noah said. He leaned back in his chair and folded his arms. 'Just forget it.'

Rex looked at the motionless zombies on screen, then back to his friend. 'You know, maybe the fair would be better than being stuck in here?'

Noah's face brightened. 'So, what, you'll come?'

'We can try,' Rex said. 'Me and Bobo have been sneaking out a lot lately, so Six has got the place locked down pretty tight. It won't be easy to get out. *Bobo!*'

There was a grunt from Rex's bed. Bobo, the talking Evo chimp, opened one eye. 'What is it, kid? I'm trying to catch up on my beauty sleep here.'

'Get your hat,' Rex told him. 'We're stepping out for some fresh air.'

Even as the hand clamped down on Rex's shoulder, he knew it belonged to Agent Six.

'And where do you think you're going?' Six asked.

Rex stood up from the air duct he had been about to crawl inside. There were few windows in Providence base, and the doors were heavily guarded. Even the ventilation system was alarmed and magnetically sealed. This should have stopped anyone breaking in or out, but Rex wasn't just anyone. His nanites had taken care of the security systems in a matter of seconds. Noah and Bobo had already clambered into the air duct. Rex could hear them thudding their way along the narrow passageway.

'Hey, Six,' Rex said, raising his voice to try to drown out the din his friends were making. He thought fast. 'We, uh, I mean *I* was just... checking the air conditioning.'

'And why were you doing that?' asked Six.

'Because,' began Rex, 'I'm thinking of becoming a... heating engineer.' He replayed the excuse in his head. 'Yeah, that works,' he said.

Six sighed. 'Bobo. Noah. Get back here.'

The thudding stopped. There was silence for a moment, and then Noah's voice echoed out from within the duct. 'Um, I don't think I can turn round.'

'Hey, get your butt out of my face, kid!' Bobo said.

'They're checking the system for blockages,' Rex explained, weakly.

'You can cut the excuses,' Six said. 'You were trying to sneak out. Again.'

Rex hung his head. 'Yeah,' he confessed. 'There's a fair in town and Noah thought it'd be cool if we went. But I know, too dangerous, I shouldn't go wandering off, *yadda, yadda, yadda*.'

He turned and spoke into the air duct. 'Come on,

guys,' he said. 'Six isn't going to let us go.'

'You can go.'

'You don't have to apologise, Six, I know it's ... Wait. Did you say I could go?'

Six nodded. 'I know being stuck in here isn't much fun, Rex, and at least this way I'll know where you are.'

Rex grinned. 'I always did like you, Six,' he said.

'But you keep your wits about you at all times,' Six instructed. 'And you're back here for curfew.'

'What time's curfew?' Rex asked.

'When I call you and tell you it is,' Agent Six said.

With a shrug, Rex clambered through the window. 'We'd better get moving, then. Thanks, Six.' Rex knelt down by the open vent.

'You know you're free to use the door now, right?' Six asked.

'Yeah, but where's the fun in that?'

Six gave him a curt nod. 'Fair enough,' he said. 'Oh, but Rex?'

'Yeah?'

'Try not to get into trouble.'

'Hey,' Rex replied, with a wink. 'I'll see what I can do!'

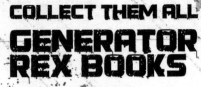